Adventures

of

Monkey King

retold by   R. L. Gao

illustrated by
Marlys Johnson-Barton

Victory Press
Monterey, CA

Copyright © 1989 by R. L. Gao

Library of Congress Cataloging-in-Publication Data

Wu, Ch'eng-en, ca. 1500 - ca. 1582
    [Hsi yu chi. English]
    Adventures of Monkey King / retold by R. L. Gao ; illustrated by
        Marlys Johnson-Barton
        p. 132 cm.
    Translation of: Hsi yu chi.
    Summary: A mischievous monkey acquires godlike powers and
        creates havoc in heaven.
ISBN 0-9620765-1-1 (pbk.) : $6. 95
    [1. Folklore -- China. 2. Monkeys -- Folklore.] I. Gao, R. L.,
    1898 -   . II. Johnson-Barton, Marlys, ill. III. Title.

PZ8.1.W9Ad   1989
895.13'46 -- dc20   89-22590
[398.2]   CIP
                                                     AC

For information contact: Victory Press
                543 Lighthouse Ave.,
                Monterey, CA 93940.
Printed in the United States of America.

ISBN 0-9620765-1-1

Table of Contents

Chapter 1

Monkey King

On the top of Mystic Mountain was a magical stone. One day this stone burst open, and a stone monkey jumped out. He could run; he could jump, and he could eat. He played with all the real monkeys on the mountain.

One hot summer day, all the monkeys were playing under the shade of an old pine tree.

"It's too hot here," cried the stone monkey. "Let's play in the stream."

He scampered off to the mountain stream with the other monkeys following. When they reached the water, everyone dived in and splashed around.

"This water's so nice and cool," said a little monkey. "But where does it come from?"

"I don't know," answered an old monkey. "Let's find out."

With that, the monkeys all dashed up the mountain along side the stream, all racing to be the first to reach the source of the water.

Near the top of the mountain, they saw a crashing waterfall.

"Who's got the guts to see what's behind the waterfall?" a big monkey challenged the others.

Nobody answered.

"If someone goes in and comes out alive, let's make him our king," the big monkey continued the dare.

"I'll go!" cried the stone monkey taking the dare.

He closed his eyes and jumped straight into the waterfall. When he opened his eyes, he found himself in a dry stone cave with stone beds, stone chairs, stone bowls and stone plates. It seemed as if everything was ready for the monkeys to live there.

The stone monkey jumped out of the cave and shouted with delight, "We're in luck!"

The other monkeys surrounded him, questioning him one after another.

"What did you see?" asked the old monkey.

"Is it big in there?" ventured the little monkey.

"What's so good about the place?" questioned the big monkey.

"Follow me and see for yourselves," replied the stone monkey.

So with a skip and a jump, he led the group of monkeys through the waterfall into the cave.

The old monkey smiled when he saw the size of the cave.

"Why, it's huge. We could all live here," he said.

"Yes, yes!" agreed the stone monkey. "We won't have to fry in the summer or freeze in the winter. We won't have to worry about wolves and tigers. We'll make this our home."

The stone monkey happily watched the little monkeys run around and the older monkeys examine the furniture and utensils.

Suddenly he called out, "Don't forget your promise!"

All heads turned to him.

"You all agreed that if I went behind the waterfall and came out alive, I should be king. I went in, came out and brought all of you into this new home. I should be king."

"That's right," declared the big monkey. "Everyone line up and bow to our new king, Monkey King."

All the monkeys readily obeyed.

From that day on, the monkeys lived a carefree existence in their new home, playing in the stream and eating fruit from the trees.

One evening while all the monkeys were drinking coconut juice, Monkey King suddenly started crying.

"What's wrong?" asked the old monkey. "Life is so pleasant now. You shouldn't cry."

"I'm sad because when we die, we'll lose all these nice things," answered the Monkey King in sobs.

The old monkey replied, "Everyone has to die. I've only heard of three types of people who never die."

"What types?" asked Monkey King eagerly.

"Buddha, fairies and spirits. These people are immortals."

"Where do these people live?" asked Monkey King.

"In fairy mountains or in heaven."

Suddenly Monkey King's spirits picked up. He grinned, "Tomorrow I'm going to go look for these people. I want to learn the secrets why they never die."

The next day Monkey King left Mystic Mountain alone. He boarded a small raft and let the wind blow him where it would.

He climbed mountains and crossed oceans, searching and searching for fairies. He asked hundreds of people but nobody could tell him anything.

Then one day while he was walking on a steep mountain path, the sound of a strange song drifted to him.

Monkey King thought to himself, "At last I've found a fairy."

He hurried to the source of the voice and found a woodcutter singing as he chopped a pile of logs.

Monkey King said politely, "Kind fairy spirit, please accept me as your student and teach me the secrets of immortality."

The woodcutter answered quickly, "You are mistaken. I'm not a fairy spirit. I'm just an old woodcutter."

"But the song you were singing sounds like a fairy song," Monkey King said in a puzzled tone.

"Oh, that song," replied the woodcutter. "My neighbor taught it to me. He's an immortal."

"So you do know an immortal! Take me to see him, please," begged Monkey King. "I've been searching for an immortal for so long."

"I'm rather busy now," said the woodcutter. "Why don't you go see him yourself? Just follow this path to the north for seven miles. When you see a cave, you'll know that's where he lives."

Monkey King followed the woodcutter's directions and indeed found a cave. But the door was shut tightly, and Monkey King dared not to knock. So he jumped up into a tree and swung in the branches, waiting for someone to come out.

After awhile, the cave door squeaked open. A little fairy boy asked, "Who's making so much racket out here?"

Monkey King greeted the fairy with a smile, "Dear fairy, I've come to learn the secrets of immortality. Please take me to see your master."

The little fairy boy led Monkey King to his master. The master was sitting on a high pedestal surrounded by little fairies.

Monkey King dropped to his knees and begged, "Dear Master Immortal, teach me the secrets of living forever."

The master asked, "Where did you come from?"

"I come from Mystic Mountain," answered Monkey. "And I've been searching all over for an immortal to teach me the secrets of living forever. Please accept me as a student."

The master agreed.

Monkey King stayed with the master for over ten years. He learned how to do a somersault and travel 18 thousand miles. He learned how to jump onto a cloud and fly to heaven. He learned how to change into any shape he wanted.

One day Monkey King and the little fairies were talking beneath a pine tree.

One fairy said, "Monkey, I heard Master has taught you all seventy-two of his secrets."

"Yes, yes!" replied Monkey grinning with delight. "He did. And I practiced every morning and every night. Now I know all his tricks."

"I don't believe it," said another fairy jealously. "Monkey, if you can change into a pine tree, then I'll believe you."

Monkey chanted a spell to himself and with a twist of his body, he suddenly disappeared and a pine tree stood in his place.

"Look at that!" cried one little fairy. "Monkey's not a monkey anymore but a tree."

The fairies all clapped their hands and laughed.

Suddenly the master came out of the cave demanding, "Who's making all this noise, disturbing my sleep?"

As Monkey changed back into his original shape, one little fairy said, "Sorry we disturbed you, Master. Monkey was just showing us the tricks you taught him."

Master pulled Monkey aside, shouting angrily, "I taught you my secrets and you go around showing off. How dare you!"

Monkey knelt before the master saying humbly, "Forgive me, Master."

Master looked unhappily at Monkey and said slowly, "I won't punish you. Just leave me and return to where you came from."

Monkey begged again for forgiveness, but Master refused. So Monkey had no choice but to return home.

Chapter 2

The Magic Rod

Monkey chanted a spell, did a somersault, and in a flash was back at Mystic Mountain. The mountain was deserted.

"Little ones, where are you?" cried Monkey King. "I have returned."

A few monkey heads peered cautiously from beneath rocks and clumps of weeds. When they saw it was their king, they ran to greet him.

"Monkey King, how come you stayed away so long?"

"Monkey King, we've been waiting for your return."

"Monkey King, an ogre threw us out of our Waterfall Cave. He captured many of our young monkeys and took them away. We tried to stop him, but he's too strong."

Monkey King said angrily, "How dare an ogre bother my subjects! I'll take care of him! Where is he?"

"We don't know," answered a frightened little monkey. "He comes and goes like a gust of wind."

"Don't be afraid," Monkey King said soothingly. "I'll show him who's boss."

Monkey King hopped on a cloud and began floating around, searching for the ogre. Soon he noticed a few little ogres guarding the front of a messy cave. When the little things saw Monkey King, they ran inside.

Monkey King shouted after them, " Tell your ogre king that I've come for revenge!"

The little ones ran inside to tell their king.

Ogre King just laughed, "What's there to be afraid of?"

He picked up his sword and walked out of the cave shouting, "Monkey King, where are you? Show your ugly face!"

Monkey retorted, "Blind ogre, can't you see? Here I am!"

Ogre King sneered, "You aren't even four feet tall. You don't have a weapon. How can you fight me?"

"Shut up and fight," cried Monkey, throwing a fist at the ogre.

The ogre blocked Monkey's fist and said with a smile, "You're so puny, I could kill you with one stroke of my sword. I'll play fair and fight fist for fist."

The ogre threw down his sword and started to fight.

After more than one hundred blows, he was panting heavily. The nimble Monkey King was too fast for him. The ogre grabbed his sword and swung at Monkey.

Monkey dodged in time to avoid injury. But in order to save himself, he needed to use a trick that his master had taught him. So Monkey plucked a hair from his body, put it in his mouth, chewed it into pieces, blew it out of his mouth and shouted, "Change!"

Immediately three hundred little monkey kings appeared from the hairs. They surrounded the ogre, pulling on his arms and legs, pinching his nose, and scratching his eyes.

Monkey took this opportunity to grab the ogre's sword and chop the ogre in two. He then rushed into the cave, killing all the little ogres and freeing all the captured little monkeys.

"Our hero!" shouted the freed monkeys joyfully. "You've saved us, Monkey King."

Monkey King grinned as he shook his body and chanted a spell. All the miniature monkey kings that

had helped in the fight immediately disappeared, returning as pieces of hair on Monkey's body.

Monkey King took the group of freed monkeys back to Mystic Mountain. He gathered everyone together and declared, "I've got to teach you all to fight. Then ogres and demons can't bully you anymore."

Everyday Monkey King trained his monkey subjects. All of them learned to punch, kick and fight with sticks. Monkey King was pleased with the progress of his subjects. But one fact bothered him.

He remarked to a group of his monkey advisors, "I need a special weapon to protect my subjects. Does anyone know where I can get one?"

"Can you get to the bottom of the ocean?" asked one advisor.

"Of course," replied Monkey King. "My master taught me all his tricks."

"Then go to the Dragon Palace at the bottom of the sea. The Dragon King has plenty of weapons. You probably can get one from him."

Monkey went to the edge of the stream, used his magic to part the water and hurried to the bottom of the ocean.

As he approached the palace, a shrimp guard blocked his way, asking sharply, "Which fairy spirit are you? Why have you come to our palace?"

Monkey King answered, "I am Monkey King of Mystic Mountain. I am a neighbor of the Dragon King. You really should recognize me."

The shrimp guard reported to the Dragon King that a neighbor had come to visit.

The Dragon King invited him in to drink tea, inquiring, "So what brings you here?"

"I'm teaching my monkey subjects to fight and protect our Waterfall Cave. But as a leader, I need a special weapon. I've heard you have many good weapons. Would you mind giving me one?"

The Dragon King didn't dare refuse. He asked a crab servant to bring out a sword.

Monkey King grabbed the sword, twirled it around his head and jabbed it into the air.

"No good!" he declared. "It's not sturdy enough."

Dragon King asked the crab servant to bring out a three-pronged pitch-fork.

Monkey King lifted it and swung it back and forth. He again cried, "No good! This one's also too flimsy."

Dragon King smiled, "But Monkey King, this pitch fork is over three thousand pounds."

"I don't like it. Get me another weapon!"

Dragon King was now frightened. He had the crab servant drag out a seven thousand pound halberd. Still Monkey King was not satisfied.

"I'm sorry, but that's all I have," the Dragon King said apologetically.

"Well, find something else," retorted Monkey.

At this point Dragon Queen came out and whispered to her husband, "Our neighbor is not ordinary. He's an immortal. Give him that piece of magic steel and get rid of him."

"But that piece of steel is so heavy, nobody possibly can move it," Dragon King returned.

Monkey overheard Dragon Queen and demanded,"Bring out this piece of magic steel and let me see."

"You'll have to go see it yourself," replied Dragon King. "Nobody can lift it. It's over thirty thousand pounds."

"Where is it? Lead me to it," cried Monkey anxiously.

Dragon King led Monkey to the middle of the ocean and pointed at a piece of glowing steel. It was over two yards long and as wide as a barrel.

Monkey walked over the heavy rod and picked it up effortlessly.

"It's a bit too thick and a bit too long. If only it were thinner and shorter it would be fine," Monkey said to himself.

Instantly, the magic rod shrunk by itself.

Monkey smiled, "Just a bit thinner and it would be perfect."

The rod indeed shrunk some more.

Monkey beamed with delight as he examined the rod carefully. It was a long black steel rod, capped with gold on both ends. It was as big as a broom handle.

Monkey twirled and spun the rod around, getting a feel for it. The crab servants and shrimp guards immediately backed off and hid from Monkey's menacing rod.

"Thank you," Monkey declared as he rested the rod on his shoulder. "It's perfect. But now that I have this weapon, I need some armor to go with it. Can you find something for me."

"I'm sorry, " replied the Dragon King. "We have nothing here."

Monkey retorted, "If you don't find some armor for me, I'm not leaving."

"Why don't you try some place else?" suggested the Dragon King calmly. "They might have something."

"I said I'm not leaving," declared the Monkey King. "I want you to get armor for me."

"If I had something, I'd certainly give it to you. But I really don't have anything."

"All right!" cried Monkey swinging his rod. "Then I'll just practice my rod techniques on you."

Dragon King replied hastily, "Please don't do that. I'll ask my brothers if they have anything."

Dragon King hit a gong and within minutes his three brothers arrived.

"What's the emergency?" asked the third brother. "Why did you hit the gong?"

Dragon King explained that Monkey King was demanding a suit of armor.

"Don't let him bully us!" cried the first brother angrily. "Let's get our armies to fight him."

"No, no, no," said Dragon King hastily. "This little monkey is dangerous. We can't win in a fight with him. It's better to give him what he wants and then report him to the Jade Emperor in heaven."

So Dragon King's brothers presented Monkey with a bright purple helmet, a golden shield and a pair of winged shoes.

Monkey King happily accepted the armor and left. But the Dragon brothers were angry.

Dragon King reported Monkey to the Jade Emperor in the Imperial Palace in Heaven.

Jade Emperor replied, "This monkey is indeed naughty, but he's also an immortal."

"You must get rid of him," begged Dragon King. "He's causing too many problems down on earth."

19

The Jade Emperor thought for a moment before replying, "I'll invite him to heaven and let him watch my peach gardens. That way he won't think I'm punishing him, and I can keep an eye on him here in heaven."

Chapter 3

Havoc in Heaven

Monkey King arrived in Heaven to take the position of Overseer of the Heavenly Peach Gardens.

Several gardeners took Monkey on a tour of the place. It was a large, spacious garden with blooming trees.

One gardener said, "These peaches were planted by Fairy Godmother. She uses them every year for her peach party."

"How many trees are there?" asked Monkey.

"Three thousand," answered the gardener. "But the peaches from this one big tree are the best. If someone eats one, he can live as long as the universe exists."

Monkey grinned when he heard this.

One day soon after his tour, Monkey King sneaked into the garden when the gardeners were not watching. He secretly ate all the peaches on the big tree. Then he climbed into the tree, changed into a two inch monkey, curled up into a ball and fell asleep.

That day Fairy Godmother happened to send seven fairy princesses to pick peaches for her party that evening. The seven princesses came into the garden with huge baskets. They went from tree to tree, picking the ripe, rosy peaches. Finally they came to the tree where Monkey was sleeping.

"Strange," remarked one princess. "This tree has no peaches."

"Isn't that one?" cried another princess pointing to the curled up Monkey King.

The first princess stood on tiptoe and stretched for the high branch to pluck off the round ball. Monkey King was jolted out of his sleep.

He immediately returned to his original size and thrashing his golden rod, shouted, "Stop stealing my peaches, you thieves!"

The princesses all cried out in fright and dropped to their knees.

One princess sobbed, "We were just following Fairy Godmother's orders. She wanted peaches for her party tonight."

Monkey suddenly smiled, "A party. I'd love to go. Who is invited?"

"Buddha, Goddess Pusa, the Barefooted Monk, the Reverend Immortal, some priests. . . "

"Did she invite me?" asked Monkey.

"We don't know."

Monkey looked at the princesses and said, "Well, I can't blame you for not knowing. But stay here while I go ask Fairy Godmother."

He chanted a spell which left all the princesses frozen like wax figures. Then he jumped on a cloud and headed for Fairy Godmother's palace.

On the way, he saw a chubby monk waddling in the same direction.

"Barefooted Monk," he cried, "Jade Emperor told me to notify everyone that the peach party will be held in his palace instead of at Fairy Godmother's."

"Really? Thank you for telling me," said a surprised Monk as he turned around and headed the other way.

Monkey King chuckled as he chanted a spell and turned into the exact image of Barefooted Monk.

"Now I can attend Fairy Godmother's party," Monkey smiled to himself.

He arrived at Fairy Godmother's palace expecting a huge crowd. But it was too early. It was deserted except for the servants setting up refreshments.

As the sweet smell of wine drifted to Monkey's nose, he said to himself, "I must taste some of that wine."

So he plucked a hair from his body and cried, "Change!"

The hair turned into a sleeping bug that flew around the room, making the servants drowsy. One by one they all dropped off to sleep.

Monkey snatched a barrel of wine and in a few gulps, finished it off.

"I'd better not let anyone catch me," he thought to himself as he quietly left the palace.

But Monkey was drunk from all his wine and couldn't find the peach garden. Instead he stumbled into the garden of the Reverend Immortal. The Immortal was busy talking to some of his students. He didn't notice Monkey sneak into his medicine room. It was filled with all sorts of strange medicines for prolonging life. Monkey picked up a small bowl of Long Life Pills.

"I'll just taste one," he said to himself, fingering the pills.

But as soon as he tasted the pills, he could not stop eating. They were so good that he finished them off like a bowl of candy.

Monkey King then thought of his subjects back in Mystic Mountain.

"They've never tasted fairy wine," he thought to himself. "They'd love this delightful drink."

So he crept back to Fairy Godmother's palace and snatched two large barrels of wine. He tucked one under each arm, jumped on a cloud and floated back to Mystic Mountain.

"Little ones!" he cried, "I've got fairy wine for us all."

"Great! Wonderful!" shouted the monkeys as they all came running out to participate in Monkey's fairy wine party.

Because of the spell cast over them, the seven fairy princesses could not move for a long time. When they finally awoke, they went straight to Fairy Godmother to tell her about Monkey King.

Fairy Godmother was irate when she heard how her princesses were bullied. She went to report the incidence to Jade Emperor.

She walked into his palace, bowed respectfully and began, "You must punish Monkey King. He's been putting evil spells on my princesses. And he stole. . ."

Just then Reverend Immortal rushed in crying, "Oh my! Jade Emperor. It's horrible! Some thief stole all my Long Life Pills."

Next, one of the servants in Fairy Godmother's palace came in addressing the emperor timidly, "Jade Emperor, somebody has taken two barrels of our fairy wine."

At this point, Barefooted Monk staggered in panting, "Emperor, did you order Monkey King to tell us that the peach party would be held here today instead of at Fairy Godmother's Palace? I walked all the way there, when Monkey told me to come here."

As Jade Emperor listened to all these complaints, his face flushed red with rage.

"Why, that irresponsible Monkey King!" he shouted angrily. "He's creating havoc in heaven!"

"Fairy General," ordered the Emperor. "Take ten thousand fairy soldiers and capture that mischievous monkey!"

Fairy General called his troops to attention and led ten thousand fairies to Mystic Mountain.

Fairy General descended in front of Waterfall Cave yelling, "Monkey King, come out and surrender or we'll kill all of your monkey race!"

The two little monkey guards standing in front of the cave immediately ran inside squeaking nervously,

"Monkey King, Jade Emperor has sent Fairy General to capture you."

Monkey King was in the midst of sipping wine with his advisors. He didn't pay any attention to the little monkeys.

After awhile another monkey guard ran in, reporting, "Monkey King, Fairy General is thrashing his sword about, cursing us all."

Monkey King continued to calmly sip his wine.

At this point another little monkey dashed in crying, "They broke down our cave door and are coming this way!"

Monkey King jumped up, shouting, "How dare they disturb my peace! Follow me, fellow monkeys!"

With that, he dashed to the entrance of the cave, running straight into Fairy General and his troops. With a swish of his rod and a few hard whacks, Monkey King sent Fairy General and his army scampering for their lives.

Back up troops rushed in to help the fleeing general. They fought all day against Monkey King and his monkeys.

When it began to get dark, Monkey King plucked a hair from his body, put it in his mouth, chewed it to pieces, blew it out and shouted, "Change!"

Instantly one thousand miniature monkey kings appeared, each carrying a golden rod. They drove Fairy General and his troops out of Mystic Mountain.

Fairy General returned to the Imperial Palace in Heaven with a few captured tigers and wolves, but without a single monkey prisoner.

"Monkey King is just too strong for us," apologized the General to the Emperor.

Chapter 4

Battle with Fairies

At this point, Goddess Pusa walked into the Imperial Palace, wondering what all the fuss was about. When she heard what was going on, she said, "Send my young nephew Prince Lang to lead the next battle."

Prince Lang, a smooth-faced young fairy boy, picked up a bow, slung a pack of arrows across his shoulder, mounted an eagle and led a group of fairies down to Mystic Mountain.

Monkey King had just organized his subjects into neat rows, ready to fight.

Prince Lang shouted, "I've come to capture you, you troublesome monkey!"

Monkey replied calmly, "You're nothing but a baby prince. I can't fight you. I don't want to hurt a baby.

Ask Fairy General and his troops to come back and fight me."

Prince Lang exploded in anger, "Just because I'm small doesn't mean I can't fight."

With that, he thrust a sword at Monkey King. Monkey King blocked with his golden rod. The two exchanged over three hundred vicious blows.

Prince Lang was determined to capture Monkey King, so he chanted a spell and grew as tall as a mountain, swinging a fist as large as a boulder at Monkey.

But Monkey was also quick. He chanted a spell and he grew as tall as Prince Lang. He waved his rod, which was now as big as a redwood tree.

When the monkey troops saw this, they all scattered in fright. Monkey King returned to his normal size and fled with his troops.

"Stop!" cried Prince Lang. "Surrender and we'll spare your measly life."

The fairy troops now rushed in upon Monkey King and encircled him.

Monkey King looked desperately on all sides. He knew he was trapped unless he used a trick. He chanted a spell, turned his golden rod to the size of a sewing needle, and put it in his ear. Then he twisted his body, changed into a sparrow, and flew to the top of a pine tree.

"He's disappeared," exclaimed the fairies.

"No, I see him!" shouted Prince Lang, throwing down his bow and arrows. He changed into a hawk in order to attack the sparrow.

Monkey quickly changed into a stork as he flew toward the water. Prince Lang then turned into a cormorant and continued the chase.

Monkey changed into a fish and he dove into the water. Prince Lang abruptly stopped in the air.

"Where did that stork go?" he asked himself. "It must be near the water somewhere."

So Prince Lang, still in the shape of a cormorant, landed on the water, waiting patiently for a clue of Monkey.

Monkey, in the shape of a fish, was swimming peacefully in the water, when he noticed that a sea bird landed in front of him. It looked like a cormorant, but the feet were not webbed.

Monkey thought to himself, "That must be Prince Lang."

So he made a quick turn and headed in the other direction.

Prince Lang sputtered, "That fish has no scales! It must be Monkey King."

Monkey heard this. He leaped out of the water, turned into a snake and hid among the wild thrush.

33

Prince Lang changed to his original form and returned to Waterfall Cave for his bow and arrows.

Monkey took this opportunity to change into an old temple. He opened his mouth like a temple door. His eyes became windows and his tongue became a statue of Buddha. Only he had no place to hide his tail, so he turned it into a flagpole at the back of the temple.

Prince Lang returned to the waterside with his weapons, but he couldn't find a trace of Monkey.

When he saw the temple, he laughed, "No temple has a flagpole at the back. That must be Monkey. I'll kick out the windows and break the statue of Buddha."

Monkey shuddered, "That Prince has seen through my disguise. Now he wants to kick my eyes and break my tongue. I'd better disappear."

So with a leap, Monkey returned to his original form and started running. Prince Lang continued the chase.

Meanwhile in Heaven, Jade Emperor, Reverend Immortal and Fairy Godmother were becoming impatient.

Goddess Pusa said, "Let's give Prince Lang a hand."

Reverend Immortal agreed, pulling out a small golden hoop from his wide sleeve. He flung it to earth, hitting Monkey on the head.

Monkey stumbled to the ground. As he got up to run again, Prince Lang and the fairy soldiers grabbed him. They tied him up with rope and led him back to heaven.

Prince Lang tied Monkey King to a stake. He used a knife to slit Monkey's throat, but the knife would not cut. He used an axe to chop off Monkey's head, but the axe would not chop. He tried a sword, a spear, fire and lighting. But nothing would kill Monkey King. Monkey had eaten too many Fairy Peaches and Long Life Pills.

Reverend Immortal was exasperated. He finally flung Monkey in a huge iron cauldron and threw on a heavy lid. He planned to boil him for forty-nine days until he turned into ash.

After forty-nine days, the Reverend Immortal opened the cauldron lid and out popped a live Monkey King. He pulled the needle from his ear and with a twirl and a chant, it grew back into the size of his golden rod.

Monkey thrashed his rod left and right, knocking over the cauldron and whacking the servants.

Reverend Immortal rushed over to stop him, but Monkey just kicked him over and rushed out of the gates of Heaven.

Jade Emperor watched in dismay as Monkey escaped. But he was at a complete loss as to how to control

Monkey. Finally he called on Buddha from the Land of Enlightenment and asked for help.

Buddha agreed. He went looking for Monkey and found him fighting a group of fairy soldiers.

"Why are you causing all this commotion?" Buddha asked calmly.

"It's my turn to rule heaven," answered Monkey. "Jade Emperor won't let me, so I'll keep bothering him until he will."

"What qualifications do you have to rule?" Buddha continued to ask.

"I know 72 tricks; I can somersault 1800 miles, and I'm an immortal. Why can't I rule heaven?" Monkey retorted.

"All right," smiled Buddha. "Prove your ability. If you can jump out of my hand with a somersault, you can rule heaven as emperor. If you can't, then you have to stay underground as a monster."

Monkey King thought to himself, "I can somersault 1800 miles. Buddha's hand is not even one foot. Of course I can win."

So Monkey King said to Buddha, "It's a deal!"

He jumped onto Buddha's hand and in a flash had somersaulted 1800 miles.

When Monkey landed he saw five reddish pillars.

"This must be the edge of the world," he thought. "I'd better put a mark here or Buddha won't believe me."

So Monkey plucked a hair from his body and cried, "Change!"

With the pen that appeared, Monkey wrote on one pillar, "Monkey King was here." Then he urinated beneath the pillar.

With another somersault he was back in front of Buddha, exclaiming, "Give the throne of heaven to me."

Buddha laughed, "Silly monkey, you didn't jump out of my hand. Look at the marks you made."

Monkey looked down at Buddha's hand. On the middle finger was written "Monkey King was here." Beneath it was a puddle of urine.

Monkey wailed, "No fair! Let me try again."

So with another leap, Monkey was in the air again. This time Buddha turned over his hand, catching Monkey. Buddha then transformed his hand into a five-ridged mountain and trapped Monkey beneath it.

Monkey could not get out. He could only peak out of a crack for air. When hungry, he ate iron and when thirsty he drank dew.

Chapter 5

Monkey King Meets Monk Tang

On earth in the city of Chang An there lived a Monk Tang. The emperor of China asked him to travel west to India to gather precious Buddhist scriptures and to bring them back to China.

After much preparation, Monk Tang, his white horse and his two monk companions began their long journey. At first, the road was wide and the travelling easy.

Late one afternoon, several months later, Monk Tang and his companions entered a dark, pathless forest. Nobody could see anything. Suddenly they all stumbled and dropped into a huge pit.

A voice boomed, "Grab them! Grab them!"

Ten ogres appeared and bound Monk Tang and his companions tightly in rope.

The hideous ogre king cried in delight, "What a feast these will make."

Monk Tang shivered at these words.

At that moment two guest ogres crawled into the pit. One guest grinned, "Why, they have prepared refreshments for us."

The ogre king ordered his servants to slice up Monk Tang's two companions and to serve them to his guests.

Monk Tang watched his companions being sliced and eaten by the ogres as they sang bawdy songs and told dirty jokes. He waited nervously for his turn.

By dawn, he nodded off to sleep from exhaustion. Suddenly, he felt someone untying his ropes.

"Please have mercy!" cried the frightened monk.

A kind old man smiled gently, "Don't worry. I won't hurt you. Last night you fell into this ogre's cave by accident. Unfortunately, your companions were eaten."

"And my horse and my luggage," continued Monk Tang.

"No, no, your horse and luggage are right here," replied the kind old man as he helped Monk Tang mount his horse.

After the old man led Monk Tang back onto a forest path, he disappeared into a wisp of clear wind and floated away.

"Praise Buddha," Monk Tang mumbled to himself. "He sent a fairy to save me."

Monk Tang continued up the steep mountain alone. Both sides of the uneven road were densely packed with huge trees. The horse gingerly made his way forward. All of a sudden, a fierce tiger appeared ahead. Monk Tang urged his horse to turn around and gallop, but the poor beast was so weary, it sank to the ground in fright.

Monk Tang put his hands together and prayed as the tiger approached.

Suddenly the tiger started, backed off and ran.

Monk Tang turned around to see a husky hunter standing behind him, wielding a large sword.

Monk Tang dropped to his knees and cried, "Kind hunter, save me from these wild beasts."

The hunter helped Monk Tang to his feet as he said, "Monk, don't be afraid. The animals in this mountain are scared of me. I'll lead you through this forest."

The hunter led Monk Tang through the dark forest, up to the top of the steep mountain.

He then turned to the monk and said, "I can't take you any further. The other side of this mountain belongs to another country. I'm not familiar with it."

Monk Tang was about to thank the hunter, when from the bottom of the mountain both heard a strange voice shouting, "Master, you've come to save me!"

Monk Tang turned pale with fright.

"Don't worry," said the hunter. "That's just a monkey who has been trapped beneath this mountain. Let's see what he wants."

The monk and the hunter descended the mountain. At the base they found Monkey King peering out.

The hunter approached Monkey and plucked off some weeds growing on his face.

"What do you want?" he asked.

"Ask my master to step up," replied Monkey.

A puzzled Monk Tang stepped foreword.

"Are you going west to get some Buddhist scriptures?" asked Monkey.

"Yes," replied Monk Tang.

"Then you're supposed to rescue me," Monkey continued. "Buddha put me under this mountain for punishment. One day when Goddess Pusa came along, I asked her to get me out. She told me if I were willing to be good and accompany a monk travelling west, I could be released from this mountain."

"But I don't have an ax or a chisel," replied Monk Tang. "I can't get you out."

"No need," cried Monkey. "As long as you are willing to accept me as your disciple, I can get out by myself."

"How?" asked the hunter.

"Go to the top of the mountain. Find the golden seal on one of the stones. If you lift the seal, I'll come out."

Monk Tang and the hunter returned to the top of the mountain and found the golden seal. Monk Tang said a prayer and began to lift the seal. A fragrant gust of wind took up the seal and blew it westward.

Monkey called from below, "Master, move away a bit so I can come out."

Monk Tang and the hunter climbed down the mountain and walked about six miles. They heard an ear-splitting creak as the mountain cracked open. In a flash, Monkey was out from under the mountain.

He ran up to Monk Tang, bowed and said, "Master, if you accept me as your disciple, I'll protect you for the rest of your journey."

Monk Tang agreed and bade the hunter good-bye.

Monkey took the reigns of the horse and led Monk Tang down the other side of the mountain.

They did not travel far when six bandits approached them, brandishing long spears and short swords.

One yelled, "Monk, leave us your luggage and horse and we'll spare your worthless life."

Monk Tang shook with fright, lost hold of the horse's reign and tumbled to the ground.

Monkey walked over to Monk Tang, helped him up and whispered, "Don't be afraid. They just want to give us some gifts."

"You must be deaf!" Monk Tang exclaimed. "They said they want our things."

"Don't worry," replied Monkey. "I can handle them."

Monkey walked over to the six bandits and shouted, "What right do you have to block this road?"

One bandit answered smugly, "We do this for a living. Leave your goods and we'll spare your life. If not, we'll smash you to bits."

Monkey laughed, "You stupid bandits don't know what's good for you. Leave your goods or I'll show you who's boss."

Upon hearing this, the bandits exploded with rage. With thrashing swords and spears, all rushed to attack Monkey.

Monkey stood calmly in the center of the circle, receiving hundreds of blows. But all bounced off him as if he were rubber.

After twenty minutes, Monkey cried, "You've all had your turn. Now it's my turn."

With that, he pulled the needle-sized magic rod from his ear, swung it until it became the size of a broom handle and thrashed it wildly, killing all six bandits within seconds.

Then Monkey strode proudly over to Monk Tang and laughed, "See! They didn't kill us. I killed them."

Monk Tang cried out, "You are now a monk. You can't just kill people."

"But they would have killed us," Monkey retorted.

"You should have scared them off. Maybe injured one or two," the monk replied. "But you had no reason to kill all six."

"When I was Monkey King, I killed hundreds of creatures," said Monkey.

"Precisely why you were put under the mountain ridge," returned the Monk. "If you're going to kill people, you can never become a monk, you evil thing."

Monkey shouted angrily, "So you think I'm not good enough to be a monk. Well then, I'll just return to Mystic Mountain and you can go West by yourself!"

With a somersault, Monkey disappeared into the clouds.

Monk Tang sighed and shook his head as he continued on his way alone.

He saw a little old lady approaching from the opposite direction and paused to let her pass. She smiled and began talking to him.

Monk Tang then told her that his disciple had left when he scolded him.

The old lady said, "My home is in the East. When I see Monkey, I'll send him back to you."

"That's very thoughtful of you," replied the monk, "But even if he returns, I'm sure he'll leave again."

"Not if you let him wear this, " said the little old lady, taking out a shiny round cap. "Chant a few lines of my magic spell and this magic cap will squeeze on his head so tightly, he won't do bad things again."

The old lady taught Monk Tang her magic chant and handed him the magic cap.

Then she turned into a wisp of golden light and headed east.

Monk Tang dropped to his knees in gratitude as he murmured, "Goddess Pusa has appeared to me and given me a magic cap."

Meanwhile Monkey went to the Dragon Palace at the bottom of the sea. He went to visit Dragon King to tell him of his latest adventures.

He boasted proudly, "Since Monk Tang doesn't want me as a disciple, I'm returning to Mystic Mountain."

Dragon King said thoughtfully, "If you return to Mystic Mountain, you'll just be a monkey king. If you go on with Monk Tang, you'll gain true enlightenment."

Monkey King listened in silence.

Dragon King continued, "Monk Tang is just trying to teach you right from wrong."

Monkey began to regret his brashness and decided to return to Monk Tang.

With a somersault, he was in front of Monk Tang exclaiming, "Let's get going!"

Monk Tang said, "We'd better eat first. There's bread in my sack."

Monkey went over to the sack and pulled out a loaf of bread. At this point he also spotted the shiny cap tucked neatly in the sack. He toyed with it for awhile and put it on his head.

Monk Tang secretly chanted the magic spell Goddess Pusa had taught him.

Monkey suddenly tumbled onto the ground screaming in pain, "Ouch! Ouch! My head! My head!"

He tried to tear the cap from his head.

Monk Tang stopped chanting.

48

Monkey grabbed his magic rod from his ear and tried to pry the cap off.

Monk Tang was afraid Monkey would tear off the cap, so he began to chant again.

Monkey turned to the monk crying, "Master, why are you cursing me? Stop, please stop."

Monk Tang asked, "Will you be good and listen to what I say?"

"Yes! Yes!" cried Monkey.

Monk Tang ceased chanting.

But as soon as he did, Monkey took his rod and aimed it at Monk Tang's head.

Monk Tang immediately began chanting again.

Monkey rolled to the ground, writhing in pain, screaming, "Stop! Stop!"

"You promise you'll be good."

"I promise! I promise!"

Monk Tang finally stopped his chanting. The two finished their dinner before continuing West.

Chapter 6

The Greedy Abbot

Monkey and Monk Tang traveled peacefully for over two months. Occasionally they met with a tiger or wolf. Early spring was beginning to show itself everywhere. The grass on the hills sprouted a tender green and the plum blossoms opened their red petals.

One evening as the sun was setting, the two came upon a large temple tucked away in the hills. A main hall occupied central position. Smaller buildings surrounded the hall.

"Why don't we stay here for the night?" Monk Tang asked Monkey as the two approached the grand building.

Monk Tang knocked on the huge wooden gate. A young monk answered. His long silk robes touched the ground as he bowed and asked politely, " Do you wish to stay here awhile? Where are you from?"

Monk Tang answered, "Yes, we'd like to stay for a night. My disciple and I are from Chang An. Our king ordered us to go to the Temple of Thunder to collect holy scriptures."

"Please come in and have some tea," invited the young monk.

He led them to the master abbot's room which was filled with a dozen young monks and the abbot.

After Monk Tang and the abbot exchanged bows, a young monk served tea in golden cups.

"These cups are beautiful," exclaimed Monk Tang as he sat himself at the table.

"Indeed, indeed!" replied the abbot with a sly smile. "But since you are from Chang An, you must also have precious objects."

Monk Tang said frankly, "I'm a travelling monk. I can't carry anything precious with me."

"But master," injected Monkey, "your purple silk robe is precious."

"How can a robe be precious?" asked one monk with a smirk. All the monks laughed.

"I've got over seven hundred silk robes," added the abbot with a sneer.

He ordered some monks to bring out his chests. They were filled with multi-colored silk robes delicately embroidered with golden thread.

Monkey looked at the robes and laughed, "They are nice, but my master's robe is even better."

At this, Monk Tang pulled Monkey to the side and whispered to him, "Don't try to show off. We are travelling alone and don't want to get into trouble. These fellows look greedy. I'm sure they'll want to take my robe once they see it."

Monkey smiled confidently, "Master, they can't do anything with me around."

Monkey then pulled out the purple robe from Monk Tang's large bundle and waved it in front of the group. A faint light glowed around the edges of the robe and gave it a magical appearance.

"Beautiful."

"Magnificent."

"Splendid."

The monks all murmured in awe.

The greedy abbot was speechless as he stared at the glowing robe in amazement. Finally he thought of a plan to get the robe away from Monk Tang.

"Kind Monk," he said, "Tonight it's too dark to see clearly. Please let me keep this with me until morning

so I can see every inch of this beautiful robe. I'll return it to you before you leave tomorrow."

"It's all your fault," Monk Tang whispered to Monkey as he reluctantly handed the robe over to the abbot.

"Thank you! Thank you!" grinned the abbot as he accepted the precious robe.

A young monk then led Monk Tang and Monkey to a small building at the front where they were to spend the night.

Meanwhile, the abbot carefully examined the purple robe.It glowed magically all by itself. Suddenly the abbot started wailing.

"Master, what's wrong?" asked a young monk anxiously.

"This robe is so exquisite, but I can only wear it for one night," moaned the abbot.

"Master if you want to wear the robe longer, just ask Monk Tang to stay longer."

"But I can't ask him to stay forever," said the abbot.

One little monk named Wisdom said with a sly smile, "I know how you can keep the robe forever."

"How?" asked the abbot eagerly.

"Well, Monk Tang and his disciple are travelling alone... and ... well, if anything should happen to them, nobody would know. So why don't we just take a knife and kill them while they are sleeping? We could bury their bodies and then the robe is ours."

"Excellent plan," cried the abbot.

"I don't think so," said an even younger monk named Planner. "The fat white-faced one will be easy to kill, but that small hairy one with the cap might escape."

"Then what should we do?" asked the abbot a bit crestfallen.

"We could surround their room with logs and start a fire," said Planner. "If anyone asks us what happened, we'll just say they weren't careful, and burned our building down, killing themselves."

"Wonderful plan," cried the abbot as he ordered all the monks to get to work moving logs.

At this time, Monk Tang was already fast asleep. But Monkey was a light sleeper. He heard the scraping and bumping of logs outside.

"What can that be?" he thought to himself. "Does somebody want to hurt us?"

He jumped up to open the door, but was afraid to wake his master. So with a twist of his body, he turned into a bee and flew out a crack in the door. With another twist, he had changed back into his original shape.

He saw a dozen young monks moving logs and dry grass around the building in which they were sleeping.

Monkey thought to himself,"Master was right. These fellows are greedy. They want to kill us and take the purple robe."

The monks had just finished moving the logs. One lit a fire at one end.

Monkey pulled the needle from his ear in exasperation and was about to swing it over his head when he thought, "If I kill these monks with my rod, Master will blame me and say I'm cruel. I'll have to use a trick for a trick."

So Monkey chanted a "Resist the Fire" spell to protect Monk Tang, the white horse and their baggage from the flames. He went to the abbot's room, snatched the magic robe and placed it on top of the abbot's roof. Then Monkey went back to the room Monk Tang was sleeping in and started blowing the flames away from his master's building toward the main hall.

Soon the central hall was blazing with bright flames. The smaller buildings also caught on fire. Monks scurried frantically about trying to save all the precious objects they had collected over the years.

The flames were so bright they woke up Black Bear Monster. He lived in Tornado Cave twenty miles away.

Black Bear thought to himself, "Morning already? I didn't sleep well last night."

He went outside to get breakfast, but saw that it was not yet daylight. Flames spurting from the nearby temple had awaken him.

"Those stupid monks are never careful," he grumbled to himself. "Now their temple is on fire. I'd better go save them."

With a jump and a leap, he landed near the abbot's room. He was about to call for water, when the purple robe caught his eye. It was glowing brightly amidst the flames.

Suddenly Black Bear forgot about the fire. "What a precious robe," he said to himself. "I can use this."

So he snatched the robe and headed back to his cave with a leap.

Chapter 7

Battle with Black Bear

The next morning the temple was a pitiful sight. Most of the buildings lay in ashes. The monks had gathered outside by the brick wall. Some were building little tents with cloth. Others were organizing the rescued objects. But most were crying.

Monkey went inside his master's room and called, "Master, time to get up."

Monk Tang arose quickly and dressed. When he went outdoors, he saw only ashes and a red brick wall.

He exclaimed, "There was a fire last night! Why didn't you tell me? Why wasn't I hurt?"

"You were sleeping and I protected you," answered Monkey."

"If you could protect me, why didn't you protect the entire temple?"

60

"Master, just like you said yesterday, those greedy monks wanted to kill you and steal your magic robe."

"So they set fire to the temple?"

"If it wasn't them, who could it be?"

"How dare you!" cried Monk Tang shaking his finger at Monkey.

"I didn't set the fire,"Monkey defended himself. But he added with a smile, "I just helped blow a little wind."

"What about the robe?" asked Monk Tang. "It's probably burned to ashes."

"No, no," replied Monkey. "I put it on top of the abbot's roof. Let's get it and be on our way."

As the two approached the abbot's room, the monks shivered. "Ghosts!" they cried in fright.

"What ghosts? Where?" exclaimed Monkey. "Stop this nonsense and return my Master's robe."

"They are still alive, even after the fire," Wisdom remarked in surprise. "They must be spirits."

The monks all got down on their knees and begged, "Have mercy on us. We didn't really want to hurt you. It was Planner and the old abbot who schemed up the idea."

"We don't want anybody's life," said Monkey irritably. "Return the robe and we'll be off."

"The abbot has it," replied one monk.

Wisdom ran ahead and cried, "Master, Monk Tang and his disciple are immortals. They didn't die in the fire last night. Return their robe, quick."

The abbot shrugged hopelessly. He had looked desperately for the magic robe but could not find it. Now he had burned his own temple to the ground. With one last mournful look at Wisdom, he charged head first into the wall, cracking his own skull and killing himself.

When Monkey entered the room, all he saw was blood spattered on the wall and a crumpled corpse.

Monkey cried, "Where did he hide the robe?"

None of the monks could answer.

"Take out every single robe in this temple and let me have a look," Monkey ordered.

All two hundred and thirty monks obediently lined up with their chests of clothing. Monkey looked through all of them one at a time, but he still could not find the purple robe.

Monk Tang finally lost his patience. "It's all your fault," he said to Monkey and began chanting his magic spell.

The cap automatically tightened on Monkey's head. Monkey fell to the ground, writhing in pain. He screamed, "Stop! Stop!"

"Do stop," cried one frightened Monk. "This is all the fault of our greedy abbot. He always found ways to collect precious objects."

"Maybe the Black Bear Monster took your robe," added another monk. "He lives in Tornado Cave to the east and often comes here to admire the abbot's valuable things."

"Maybe," replied Monkey. "I'll go have a look. There's nothing here."

"And you monks listen to me. Bury this greedy corpse, watch my master and feed my horse."

"Yes, yes," replied the monks in chorus.

"If you don't do as I say..." Monkey took the needle from his ear, swung it until it was as long as a broom and struck the red brick wall. The wall crumbled to the ground. "...you'll have a taste of my rod."

"Have mercy," begged an old monk falling to his knees. "Of course we'll follow your orders."

Then with a somersault, Monkey headed toward Tornado Cave. He landed near the entrance. On the grass in front of the cave he saw a shaggy black bear, talking to a thin priest and a young student. He overheard the bear say, "Tomorrow is my mother's birthday. Last night I found a magic Buddhist robe. I'm going to present that to her at her party."

"So you stole my robe!" Monkey cried as he brandished his rod and ran toward the group. The bear disappeared into the cave. The priest jumped on a cloud and was gone. But Monkey killed the student with one blow of his stick.

Monkey then ran to the front of the cave and pounded on the locked door.

"Return my Master's robe or you'll pay for it with your life," he cried.

"What kind of monk are you?" retorted Black Bear Monster as he dressed in armor in preparation for a fight.

"Just hand over the robe," cried Monkey, "Or I'll smash your cave."

With a long deep growl, Black Bear rushed out of the cave with his long spear. He jabbed menacingly at Monkey. With great agility, Monkey blocked and returned a blow with his rod.

The two exchanged blows for over an hour. Black Bear suddenly said, "Let me take a break. I'll fight with you after lunch."

"What a wimp!" cried Monkey. "Nobody with any guts eats in the midst of a fight. Let's fight to the finish."

Monkey threw a blow with his rod. The bear blocked and quickly disappeared into his cave. After he

securely locked his doors, he called his little bears together to prepare the birthday party for his mother.

Monkey pounded on the cave door for a while, but got no answer. He finally grew impatient and returned to the temple to tell Monk Tang the news.

"Master," cried Monkey flying in on a cloud. "The monks were right. Black Bear Monster stole your magic robe. But he's eating lunch now and won't fight."

"Have some lunch, too," Monk Tang replied. "At least we know where the robe is."

Monkey impatiently ate a few fruits before rushing back to Tornado Cave. On the way, he spotted a little bear carrying something. With one swing of his rod, he smashed the bear as flat as a pancake and grabbed the piece of paper. It was an invitation which read: "Master Abbot, you are invited to a birthday party for my mother. Tomorrow noon."

Monkey laughed, "So the greedy abbot and this Bear Monster were in cahoots. But the bear does not know that the old abbot is dead. Now with this invitation, I have a method to get my master's robe back."

Monkey chanted a spell and changed into the form of the greedy old abbot. He knocked on the door of Tornado Cave. Black Bear answered.

"I see you are having a party for your mother," said Monkey. "What will you give her as a gift? May I see?"

Black Bear replied, "Master Abbot, I just sent off the messenger with the invitation. How did you get here so fast?"

"I was taking a walk," Monkey fibbed, "when I met your messenger. He gave me the invitation directly."

"But how did you know that I want to give my mother a gift?" asked the bear a bit perplexed.

Monkey was about to make up an answer when a young bear come rushing into the cave.

"Disaster!" he cried. "The messenger to Master Abbot has been killed. His body is lying by the side of the road as flat as a pancake. Monkey King has probably changed into the shape of the abbot and is trying to get the robe."

Black Bear immediately grabbed his spear and before Monkey could get his rod from his ear, Black Bear had chased him out of the cave and locked the doors.

Monkey pounded on the doors for with his fists. Then he hacked at the door with his rod, but nothing happened.

Suddenly Monkey had an idea. With a somersault he was up in heaven. He gave Goddess Pusa a bow and asked,"Will you help me get Monk Tang's robe?"

Pusa said with a smile, "Monkey, nobody would have taken that robe if you were not trying to show off."

"But Goddess Pusa, if I don't get that robe, Monk Tang can't continue on his journey."

"All right," Pusa agreed. "I'll help you for Monk Tang's sake."

The two boarded a cloud and headed toward Tornado Cave. They saw a thin priest heading in the same direction. He was carrying a crystal plate with two Long Life Pills.

With one swing of his rod, Monkey smashed the priest's head and killed him.

"Why you cruel Monkey!" exclaimed Pusa. "He did not steal your robe, why did you kill him?"

"Because he's friends with that thief-of-a-bear. I saw them talking yesterday," Monkey replied. "Besides I have a plan."

Monkey asked Pusa to change into the shape of the priest. He changed himself into the shape of a Long Life Pill.

"When Black Bear eats me," Monkey chuckled "I'll give him all sorts of stomach pains until he hands over the robe."

Pusa agreed that Monkey had a good plan. She put Monkey on the crystal plate, smoothed out her priest robes and knocked on the door of Tornado Cave. Black Bear invited the priest in.

"I've got a birthday present for your mother, Long Life pills," Pusa said.

"Thank you," replied the bear.

"There are two pills. Why don't you try the big one first?" Pusa said pointing to the Monkey pill.

Black Bear eagerly swallowed the pill. As soon as Monkey slid down into Black Bear's stomach, he jumped up and down, kicked and punched and made a lot of noise.

The bear doubled over at the waist and rolled to the ground groaning in anguish.

"Stop! Stop!" he cried.

"Where is the magic robe?" Pusa asked.

"Get ... get ... the robe," Black Bear gasped to a young bear.

The young bear hurried off and returned with the magic robe. He handed it over to Pusa. At this moment, Monkey shot out through Black Bear's nose. He took the robe, thanked Pusa, and hurried back to Monk Tang.

Chapter 8

Piggy

Monk Tang and Monkey continued on their journey west. One night about a week later, the two entered a small village. They saw a youth in straw sandals rush out of a thatched cottage.

Monkey greeted him with a wave, "Hello, what is the name of this village?"

The youth shifted the pack on his back and continued walking as he answered, "Why ask me? There are dozens of people in this village."

"Why be so rude?" asked Monkey. "I just asked a simple question."

When the youth ignored Monkey and hurried on his way, Monkey grabbed his arm and would not let go.

"My master always takes his anger out on me," cried the youth, "and now you are too."

"Just answer my question," said Monkey.

"This is the Gao Village. Almost everyone's last name is Gao."

Monkey still did not release his grip on the youth.

"Let go!" cried the youth in agitation.

"Why are you in such a hurry?" asked Monkey, tightening his grip on the youth.

"I'll tell you if you let me go," winced the youth in pain.

"Let him go. Let's ask somebody else," said Monk Tang.

But Monkey would not let go. So the youth began talking.

"My master's name is Mr. Gao. His youngest daughter is so ugly nobody would marry her. Three years ago a strange looking fellow with big ears and a broad nose married her. When Mr. Gao found out he was some sort of demon, he tried to get rid of him. But the demon took the daughter and locked her up in the back shed with himself."

"Mr. Gao told me to find a powerful monk with magical powers to get rid of the demon. But the last three monks have been useless. That demon still has a grip over Mr. Gao's daughter. Mr. Gao says it is all my fault that I can't find a monk who can exorcise the demon."

"I was just on my way to find another monk when you came by and delayed me," the youth replied hurriedly.

"Now let me go so I can be off."

Monkey dropped the youth's arm and declared, "I'm just the monk you are looking for. Go back and tell you master you need not travel far."

"I hope you're not joking," said the youth. "I don't need to get in any more trouble."

"I guarantee my magical powers," said Monkey with confidence.

The youth led Monk Tang and Monkey to the front door. He went in to call Mr. Gao, but bumped right into him as he was coming out.

"You lazy fool!" cried the old man. "I told you to look for a monk."

"There are two outside the front door," the youth replied.

Mr. Gao hurried to greet them.

"Masters, welcome," he said with a bow.

Monk Tang returned the bow, but Monkey just stood and grinned.

Mr. Gao turned to the youth and whispered hoarsely, "I already have a pig-faced son-in-law who I can't get rid of. Now you bring in this hairy ape and call him a monk. He'll probably be the death of me."

Monkey retorted, "Old Mr. Gao, if you judge people only on appearance, you are wrong. I may be ugly, but I am powerful. I have the ability to get rid of your troublesome son-in-law."

Mr. Gao was embarrassed that Monkey overheard what he said. But he quickly regained his composure and led Monkey and Monk Tang indoors.

"Where are you from?" asked Mr. Gao.

Monk Tang answered, "We are from Chang An and we are going to Thunder Temple in the west to get Buddhist sutras. We hope to stay here one night."

"Oh, so you really want lodging," returned Mr. Gao. "You don't know how to catch demons."

"Catching demons and spirits is easy," laughed Monkey. "How many do you have?"

"How many?" cried Mr. Gao. "One is enough. That son-in-law of mine."

"Tell me more about him," said Monkey.

"I have three daughters," said Mr. Gao. "So I was hoping that my youngest son-in-law would move in with me to help me with the farming in my old age. Three years ago a fellow with the surname of Boar came by. He could plow and he could hoe. He had so much strength he didn't need the help of a horse."

"His only problem is that he looks like a pig. His ears are big and his nose is broad and flat. And he eats like a pig too. He eats three to five pounds of rice a meal!"

"Since he works so much, he has to eat," said Monkey.

"Luckily he's a vegetarian. If he ate meat, he'd eat me out of house and home. But it's not his eating that bothers me," Mr. Gao added hastily, "It's the fact that he flies around on clouds and can create wind and rain. Now the neighbors have all been talking about me behind my back."

"If that's all he does," declared Monkey, "Then he'll be easy to catch."

"But he's locked my daughter up in the back shed."

"I can get her out safely," Monkey assured Mr. Gao.

As Mr. Gao served the two dinner, he asked, "Do you need any weapons? I have swords and spears."

Monkey replied, "I have my own."

"I don't see anything," returned Mr. Gao.

Monkey pulled the needle from his ear, swung it until it was as long as a broom handle and showed the shiny rod to Mr. Gao.

"Well, then do you need any helpers?"

"Yes, invite a few people over to talk with my Master until I catch the demon."

After dinner, Mr. Gao seated Monk Tang with several of his neighbors and left them chatting comfortably. Then he led Monkey to the shed at the back of the house. The shed was secured with a heavy iron lock. With his rod, Monkey smashed the lock to pieces and the door squeaked open. Inside was pitch dark.

"Call your daughter," Monkey said to Mr. Gao.

Mr. Gao took a deep breath to control his shaking knees, then he whispered into the dark room," Little one, are you there?"

"Daddy? I'm here," replied a weak voice. A thin pale girl ran forward and hugged her father.

"Where's the demon?" asked her father anxiously.

"I don't know. He leaves at dawn every morning and returns around midnight," replied the sobbing girl. "After he heard you wanted to get rid of him, he's never at home."

"Now, now, there, there," said Monkey. "Don't cry. Go with your father. I'll take care of the demon."

Mr. Gao led his daughter back to the thatched cottage. Monkey twisted his body and chanted a spell. Immediately he changed into the shape of young Miss Gao. He crawled into bed and patiently waited.

Around midnight, Monkey heard a gust of wind and with it a demon flew into the shed. He had a fat round face with big ears and a broad flat nose.

Piggy jumped into bed, not realizing Monkey King was there in place of his wife. He hugged Monkey and was about to kiss him when Monkey grabbed his nose and pinched it.

"Ouch," cried Piggy. "Are you mad at me, dearie?"

"You were out in those clothes all day. They're dirty," Monkey said in his sweetest voice. "Go change."

Piggy got up to change clothing. Monkey sneaked out of bed and sat on a chair. Piggy crawled back into bed and called, "Dearie, where did you go? Come to bed."

Monkey replied with a long sigh, "My parents cursed me today because of you."

"Why?"

"They say you are never around. You are always flying off with the wind. The neighbors are laughing at us for being so stupid. My father wants to ask a monk to get rid of you."

Piggy laughed, "Don't worry. I can handle any monk. I have a nine-pronged hoe that can kill anyone."

"My father is getting Monkey King to capture you."

Suddenly Piggy sat up in bed. "I'd better leave! That Monkey King is vicious. I heard he fought a battle with Fairy General and won."

Monkey twisted his body and chanted a spell. He changed back into his original form, crying "Look here, you demon. Who am I?"

Piggy turned around and saw Monkey King grinning at him.

Piggy jumped on a gust of wind and was off. Monkey leaped on a cloud and was close at his heels, shouting, "You can't escape from me. If you go to heaven, I can follow you. If you go to hell, I can still follow you."

Piggy landed on top of a high mountain and dived into a huge cave, locking the door behind himself.

Monkey charged at the door with his magic rod and smashed the door to pieces. Piggy grabbed his nine-pronged hoe and rushed toward Monkey, yelling, "You have no right to break down my door."

"And you have no right to hold Miss Gao hostage!" returned Monkey brandishing his rod.

"Mr. Gao agreed to the marriage," cried Piggy angrily as he stabbed at Monkey with his hoe.

Monkey blocked and said with a laugh, "That isn't a weapon. You can only plant tomatoes and cucumbers with that."

"I've killed hundreds of demons with this," retorted Piggy.

Monkey suddenly lowered his rod. "I'll let you chop off my head with it and you'll see it's useless."

Monkey stretched out his neck allowing Piggy to thrust the hoe into his head. Nothing happened.

Monkey grinned, "When I was in heaven, I ate Long Life Pills and Long Life Peaches. Now nothing can kill me."

Piggy exclaimed with exasperation, "I know you are the famous Monkey King. But *what* are you doing *here?*"

"I am accompanying Monk Tang, my Master, to Thunder Temple in the west to collect Buddhist sutras. We stopped at Mr. Gao's house for the night and he asked me to capture you and rescue his daughter."

Suddenly Piggy dropped to his knees and bowed his head respectfully. He begged, "Take me to see your master."

"Why do *you* want to see him?"

"Goddess Pusa is punishing me. I am supposed to be a farmer here until a monk comes along. The monk will save me from this farm and take me west."

Monkey thought to himself. "This demon really is afraid of me. He sure can make up a good story to try to escape."

"Why didn't you tell me you were travelling with Monk Tang?" asked Piggy ruefully.

"How do I know you aren't lying?" asked Monkey.

"I swear, I am telling the truth," said Piggy.

"I'll believe you if you burn down your cave."

Indeed, Piggy set fire to his home and calmly watched it burn to ashes.

"Okay, now take me to Monk Tang," said Piggy.

"Give me your hoe."

Piggy handed over his hoe.

Monkey thought to himself. "This fellow *is* telling the truth."

So he grabbed Piggy by one ear and cried, "Hurry up. Let's go."

"Not so tight," Piggy winced, "You're hurting my ear."

Soon Monkey led Piggy into Mr. Gao's cottage and pointed to Monk Tang, "That's my master."

To the surprise of Mr. Gao and the two old neighbors, Piggy quickly dropped to his knees in front of Monk Tang and cried, "Master, your disciple is waiting for your orders."

"Monkey," said a perplexed Monk Tang, "How did you get the demon to surrender and call me master?"

"He did it on his own," Monkey said as he related what had just happened.

"However it happened," exclaimed Mr. Gao, "You deserve a reward. You can have half of my farming land. You can have one hundred ounces of gold. Whatever you want."

"One night's lodging and some food to take on our journey is all that we need," replied Monk Tang. "We are traveling to get Buddha's sutras. We don't need anything else."

Chapter 9

Yellow Wind Cliff

The next morning Monk Tang, Monkey and Piggy set out West.

One evening after three days of traveling, the group came to the foot of a steep mountain.

"Let's rest first and then continue," said Monk Tang.

"Good idea," replied Piggy, "I'm starving. A nice meal would give me more energy to carry the baggage."

"You've only been travelling three days and you're complaining already," remarked Monkey.

"I can't drink dew and eat sunlight like you can," replied Piggy. "All this walking is strenuous."

"I'm sorry to hear that," said Monk Tang. "Maybe you are not fit to be a monk. You better return to Mr. Gao's house."

"No, no, master," Piggy replied. "I was just a bit hungry. After eating, I'll be fine. Besides, there's a house right next to that clump of trees."

As the three approached, they noticed an old man on the front porch reciting Buddhist scriptures to himself.

Monk Tang asked, "May we have lodging for a night?"

The old man replied, "Where are you going?"

"We are going west to get Buddhist sutras from Thunder Temple."

"Oh don't go west, go east," said the old man.

Monk Tang looked puzzled. "But Goddess Pusa told me to come west."

Monkey exploded, "Old man, don't lie to us. If you don't have room for us to stay the night just say so. We can always sleep beneath the trees! Just don't give us wrong directions."

At this moment two youths carrying hoes and an old lady with a basket came up to the house from the fields. When they spotted a white horse and luggage, they hurried forward to see what was going on.

Piggy turned around, flapped his large ears like birds' wings and snorted loudly through his nose.

One youth dropped his hoe in surprise. The other cried, "Demons!" The old lady fell over in fright.

Monk Tang helped the old lady to her feet and explained,"Don't be afraid of my disciples. They are just tired from travelling."

The old man reluctantly led everyone indoors. He went to the kitchen to prepare dinner.

Monk Tang quitely chastised his disciples. "You both need to behave better. Your appearance already scares people. But when you speak and act so crudely, people are offended."

"But I look better than before," Piggy replied. "I have already lost weight from all this walking."

"You would look even better if you pressed your ears against the back of your head and tucked your chin in," laughed Monkey.

The old man soon served dinner. He and Monk Tang chatted awhile before Monk Tang asked, "Why did you tell me not to go west?"

"The mountain in front of us is called Yellow Wind Cliff. There are many dangerous monsters on that hill. Nobody has reached the other side alive."

While the others were talking and eating slowly, Piggy had already finished all the food on the table. The elderly man returned to the kitchen and brought out the food remaining in the pots. Piggy finished that food in two mouthfuls.

"Cook some more," Piggy complained. "I'm not even half full."

The old man cooked two large pots of rice. Piggy ate it all by himself and declared that he was still hungry.

As the old man returned to the kitchen a third time, Monk Tang declared with embarrassment, "Enough, enough."

Piggy reluctantly stopped eating.

The next morning as the three set off, the old man cautioned them to be very careful of the monsters. Monkey waved off his warnings as he led the group up the cliff. Monk Tang followed on the white horse and Piggy brought up the rear with the baggage.

About noon, a strong gust of wind blew towards them, carrying little pebbles and sand.

Piggy called out, "Let's stop and hide from that terrible wind."

"If you are scared of a little wind, what will you do about monsters?" snickered Monkey as he ignored Piggy's request and continued up the cliff.

Unexpectedly, a spotted tiger charged at them from the side. Monk Tang took one look at the ferocious beast and tumbled off his horse in fright.

Piggy grabbed his nine pronged hoe and rushed at the tiger crying, "Who are you?"

The tiger stood up on his two hind legs, thrashed the claws of his forelegs wildly about and shouted, "I am the vanguard of the King of Yellow Wind Cliff! I am out hunting for the king's lunch."

The tiger sprang for Piggy with the remark, "You do look tasty."

Piggy blocked with his hoe and forced the tiger to retreat down the side of the cliff.

Monkey meanwhile helped Monk Tang to his feet and said, "Master, wait here. I'll help Piggy kill the tiger, and we'll be on our way."

In a flash Monkey was at Piggy's side, thrashing his rod wildly. The tiger knew he was outnumbered. He rolled behind a large tree, unzipped his skin, peeled it from his body and placed it on a rock. Leaving this disguise to fool the two, he flew back up the mountain and grabbed Monk Tang.

The tiger vanguard returned to the cave of the Tiger King. He presented Monk Tang to his leader, saying "King, I got your lunch."

"He looks tasty," replied Tiger King. "Bind him up and save him for dinner. I'm not hungry now."

Meanwhile, Piggy and Monkey were searching for the tiger. Monkey spotted tiger fur near a tree and gave

it a heavy whack with his rod. A sharp pain shot up his arm. Piggy hit the fur with his hoe and dented one prong.

"Oh no!" cried Monkey. "We fell for his trap. He's left his skin on a rock and disappeared. I bet he captured Master."

Monkey and Piggy both flew back to the top of the cliff. Indeed the white horse stood alone.

"Oh dear! Oh dear!" moaned Piggy. "What *shall* we do?"

"Watch the horse and baggage while I search the mountain," declared Monkey.

Monkey flew up on a cloud and scanned the mountain. He found a cave with a sign hanging over it which read "King of Yellow Wind Cliff."

Monkey leaped down in front of the cave and pounded on the door, shouting, "You idiot tiger! If you know what's good for you, you'll hand over my Master."

Tiger King looked at his tiger vanguard unhappily, "I told you to get me some lunch. Why did you take this fat monk with such a fierce disciple? Now what shall I do?"

"Don't worry," replied the vanguard. "Leave everything to me. I can capture that hairy ape for your dessert!"

The tiger vanguard collected fifty little tiger soldiers and rushed out of the cave yelling, "What do you want, you hairy ape?"

"What do *I* want?" exclaimed Monkey in irritation. "You kidnapped my master and then ask what *I* want? Return my master and I'll spare your life. If not, you will get a taste of my magic rod!"

"Tiger King will have you for dessert tonight," cried tiger vanguard.

Monkey gritted his teeth, his eyes blazing with anger. With one stroke of his rod, he injured the vanguard's foreleg. The fifty little tigers all fled in fright.

The vanguard escaped up the side of the cliff. After he had boasted to his king about his ability, he did not dare return to the cave without Monkey.

With Monkey close on his heels, the vanguard ran through the rocks and weeds. Soon he was panting and gasping up the top slope.

Piggy was sitting calmly with the horse, when he heard a gasping sound behind him. He turned around and saw the tiger vanguard a few feet ahead of Monkey. With one swift sweep of his nine-pronged hoe, he knocked the tiger to the ground. Blood oozed from nine holes and the tiger grew limp.

"Good work, Piggy," grinned Monkey. "Although that idiot tried to escape from me, he couldn't get away from you. Good work."

"I'll go back and get Master. You stay with the horse," said Monkey as he picked up tiger vanguard's body and dragged it back down the slope.

Meanwhile the little tiger soldiers filtered back into the cave one by one.

"Tiger King," replied one soldier, "Monkey King is too strong for the vanguard. He killed him on top of the slope."

Tiger King exploded in anger, "I did not eat that fat Monk Tang and that Monkey kills my vanguard. He'll pay for this!"

Tiger King put on a helmet, picked up his shield and grabbed a long pitch fork. He rushed out to face Monkey King.

Monkey was standing on tiger vanguard's body, swinging his magic rod calmly. When he saw Tiger King, he shouted, "Hand over my Master."

Tiger King took one look at Monkey's tiny frame and burst out laughing, "You are such a dinky little thing. How can you fight?"

"I may be small, but I am powerful," returned Monkey angrily as he attacked with his rod.

Soon the two were engaged in heated battle, thrusting, stabbing, jabbing, swinging, hacking, chopping, but all to no avail. For each blow there was a block. For each block there was a new blow.

Monkey finally decided to use his magic tricks. He plucked a hair from his body and blew on it, crying "Change!" Instantly one hundred little Monkey Kings appeared, each wearing his own magic cap and each wielding his own magic rod. They quickly surrounded Tiger King and attacked.

Tiger King took a deep breath, puffed up his cheeks and blew at the ground. Suddenly a yellowish wind blew up from the ground. It was cold and piercing. It blew all the little Monkeys into the air like balloons.

Monkey gasped in surprise. He shook his body, chanted a spell and collected back all the little monkeys onto his body. Brandishing his rod, he charged at Tiger King. This time Tiger King took another deep breath and blew straight into Monkey's eyes.

The wind was deadly. Monkey's eyes burned with pain. He could not see, so he backed off and fled. Tiger King did not chase him, but returned to his cave.

Monkey finally found Piggy with the horse hiding beneath some trees.

"Did you feel that yellow wind?" asked Piggy. "It's vicious."

"Tiger King blew the wind into my eyes. Now I can't see. We have to find an eye doctor," said Monkey squinting at Piggy as tears dripped from his eyes.

The two followed the mountain path until they were almost half way down the other side. Piggy finally saw the light a light shining from a farm hut.

Monkey approached the elderly farmer and asked, "Do you know of any eye doctors around here?"

"Why do you need an eye doctor?" asked the old farmer.

"Tiger King blew his wind into my eyes and now I can barely see."

"Please don't tell lies," said the old farmer. "Tiger King's yellow wind is so deadly, if he blew it into your eyes, unless you are an immortal, you would be dead by now."

"I am not quite an immortal," replied Monkey King. "But I learned some tricks from immortals."

"There are no eye doctors around here, but I do have a salve that might work. Come in and have some dinner. After dinner, put some of this on your eyes and go to sleep. Tomorrow your eyes should be cured."

When the sun rose the next morning, Monkey stretched, opened his eyes and looked around."That medicine works wonders," he thought to himself. "I see better than before."

When Piggy got up, both returned to Yellow Wind Cave. Piggy waited in the bushes with the horse while Monkey approached the cave.

A little tiger guard was snoring at the entrance. Monkey chanted a spell and changed into the shape of a mosquito. He bit the tiger on the nose before squeezing in through a crack in the door.

Monkey flew throughout the entire cave without finding Monk Tang. Finally he flew out the back door into the court yard. He found Monk Tang bound to a post, weeping quitely.

Monkey alighted on Monk Tang's head and whispered, "Master, don't cry."

"Monkey? Where are you?" asked Monk Tang in surprise.

"I am on your head. Don't worry, I'm here to save you."

Just then, both heard a little tiger say, "Tiger King, this morning as I went out on patrol, I saw the pig hiding in some bushes, but I did not see Monkey King. You must have killed him last night with your wind."

Another little tiger replied, "If he's dead, that's great. But what if he went to get help from some spirits?"

Tiger King laughed, "I am not afraid of any spirits, that is, except for the Good Fairy. But that stupid Monkey will never think of getting help from the Good Fairy."

Monkey thought to himself, "I don't know where the Good Fairy lives, but I'll find out."

"Master, I'll be back," Monkey whispered as he flew out of Yellow Wind Cave and changed back into his original form.

He flew up to heaven and found an old man spirit who was out for a stroll, "Where does the Good Fairy live?"he asked.

"She lives 3000 miles to the north, on top of Fairy Mountain," replied the spirit.

With a somersault, Monkey was on top of Fairy Mountain. The mountain was surrounded by fluffy white clouds and a fragrant breeze whispered through the willow trees.

Monkey bowed to a group of priests sitting beside the trees. "Please tell me, is this the Good Fairy's home?" asked Monkey politely.

"Yes, why do you need to see her?"

"I want her help in seizing Tiger King of Yellow Wind Cliff. He's captured my master."

At this moment a beautiful fairy dressed in flowing white robes appeared. "Monkey King, I am sorry what

happened to your Master. I am in charge of Tiger King and I see he is misbehaving. I will help you capture him."

Good Fairy picked up a black walking cane in the shape of a dragon. Then she and Monkey King floated down to Yellow Wind Cliff on a white cloud.

Good Fairy said, "Monkey, you get Tiger King to come out."

Monkey leaped off the cloud and landed in front of the cave entrance, shouting, "Tiger King, return my Master or come out and fight!"

Tiger King rushed out with his pitch fork, ready to attack. Good Fairy dropped the dragon walking cane. The dragon came alive as it floated down to earth and caught Tiger King with its claws.

Monkey rushed forward with his rod and was about to smash Tiger King, when Good Fairy landed on the ground. "Don't hurt him," she said as she helped Tiger King to his feet. "I have to take him to Buddha to be punished. Go save Monk Tang."

Good Fairy led Tiger King away. Monkey hurried into the cave, untied Monk Tang and joined Piggy. The three then continued on their journey west.

Chapter 10

Sandy

Monk Tang, Monkey, and Piggy climbed down the other side of Yellow Wind Cliff. They travelled peacefully for several months. As the signs of autumn blew in the air, they came to a large, flat plain. Crickets chirped in the grass and the willow trees were beginning to lose their leaves. Suddenly they came upon a large expanse of water which blocked their path.

Monk Tang drew in the reins of the horse and sighed, "I don't see a boat or raft. How will we cross this river?"

Monkey jumped into the air, cupped his hand over his eyes and peered around. The water in the river churned turbulently.

"Master," he said, "this river is huge. If you want me to cross it, I could do it in a somersault, but I don't know how you can get across."

"I can't see the other side," said Monk Tang. "How wide is it?"

"At least eight hundred miles," returned Monkey.

Suddenly the three heard a loud splash. A thin, dark-faced creature shot out of the river and lunged toward Monk Tang. Monkey grabbed Monk Tang and dragged him up the bank. Piggy brandished his nine-pronged hoe and rushed at the human-like monster. The creature attacked Piggy with a long black walking cane.

Monkey moved Monk Tang, the horse and the luggage to a safe place. He watched anxiously as Piggy and the creature battled furiously on the shore of the river.

"Piggy needs some help," he said to Monk Tang as he charged toward the bank swinging his magic rod. When the creature saw that Monkey was about to attack, he turned around and dived back into the river.

"Monkey!" cried Piggy with irritation. "I almost got him. If you hadn't scared him away I could have captured him."

"I couldn't let you have all the fun," laughed Monkey. "I haven't used this rod since we captured the Tiger King. My feet were getting itchy for a fight."

The two returned to Monk Tang in good spirits.

"The creature gave up," grinned Monkey. "He doesn't want to fight."

"That creature has probably lived here for a long time," said Monk Tang thoughtfully. "If you can capture him, he might be able to tell you where to find a boat or how to cross this river."

Piggy chuckled, "Monkey, since you want to fight, you go catch him."

"Well, to tell you the truth," Monkey said modestly "I'm not that skilled in fighting in the water. If you want me to do anything on land, I have no problem. You name the trick, I can do it."

"I can fight him in the water, one on one," said Piggy. "But what if he's got a whole army of thin, dark-faced creatures down there? They'll beat me within a minute."

"Go into the water and fight. Then pretend you are defeated. Let him chase you onto the bank. I will handle him from there," said Monkey.

Piggy dived into the river with his hoe. The creature was resting at the bottom of the river. When he saw Piggy, he attacked savagely with his cane. The two thrashed and splashed, churning up the water and creating waves.

Monkey watched the water anxiously. Suddenly he heard Piggy panting. First the tip of a hoe emerged on the surface of the water. Then Piggy's head appeared. Finally the creature came forth.

As Piggy swam toward the bank, Monkey grabbed his rod and flew toward the river. When the creature saw Monkey, he abruptly turned around and dived back into the water.

"Why so fast?" cried Piggy dripping with water. "Why didn't you wait until I had him on land? Now he'll never come out again."

"Besides," Piggy added, "If you can fly so easily, why don't you just pick Master up and fly across the river with him?"

"Well, why don't you just swim across the river with Master on your back?" retorted Monkey.

"Because he's human. Human beings are too heavy," replied Piggy.

"The same for me," said Monkey. "I can fly, but I can't carry a human with me."

"How will I cross the river?" asked Monk Tang quietly.

"Let me go ask Goddess Pusa. If she wants us all to go west to get those Buddhist sutras, then she will have to help us cross this river," Monkey replied.

"But how long will it take you to get to Goddess Pusa?" asked Piggy.

"I can get there and back in a few minutes," said Monkey as he did a somersault and was off.

Monkey landed on Putuo Mountain and met Goddess Pusa. "You must help me. Monk Tang can't get across a wide river and there's a vicious creature in the water who fights with Piggy."

Pusa smiled, "Monkey, that creature is your companion. He has been waiting in Flowing Sand River for a long time. He is suppose to join you on your journey west to atone for his crimes. Why didn't you ask for his help?"

"He attacked us," cried Monkey. "And he didn't say anything about coming west."

Pusa gave Monkey a red gourd and said, "Use this gourd as a boat to ferry Monk Tang across the water. Call 'Sandy' and he'll come out of the water to help you."

Monkey somersaulted back to Flowing Sand River and called "Sandy, Sandy."

The dark-faced creature was resting at the bottom of the river when he heard someone call his name.

He thought to himself, "That must be Pusa calling me to join Monk Tang."

He straightened out his disheveled robes, polished his bald head and came to the surface of the water, calling, "Where is my Master?"

He spotted Monkey holding the gourd and cried, "Why it's you, you vicious Monkey. What do you want?"

"I am also Monk Tang's disciple. You'll be travelling with me and Piggy."

"If I have to travel with you, then I am not going," declared Sandy.

"We don't want you anyway," shouted Piggy from the banks.

"Stop fighting," ordered Monk Tang.

Sandy looked to the bank and saw Monk Tang sitting calmly, a gentle smile spread on his kind face. Sandy immediately went up to him and bowed, saying, "Master, I will do as you say."

"We need to cross the river," said Monk Tang.

Sandy took the red gourd, placed it in the river and asked Monk Tang to sit inside. Then he got in front of the boat and pulled it through the water. Piggy swam along side and Monkey brought up the rear, leading the horse. Within minutes, the boat safely reached the other side of the river.

Chapter 11

The Magic Fruit Tree

Monk Tang, Monkey, Piggy and Sandy travelled along the plains. Soon they reached a high mountain. A small brook trickled down the side and exotic trees grew everywhere.

"The scenery is lovely," exclaimed Monk Tang. "We must be close to Thunder Temple."

"We're far from it," laughed Monkey, "We still have eighteen hundred miles to go."

"Even so," remarked Sandy, pointing to the top of the mountain, "There's a beautiful temple."

The four were looking at Longevity Temple on Longevity Mountain. Reality Spirit lived in Longevity Temple. He had planted a magic fruit tree in his court yard. Every three thousand years the tree would bloom. Three thousand years later thirty magic fruit would start to grow. After three thousand more years the fruit would ripen. It would take ten thousand years before anyone could eat the fruit.

The fruit grew in the shape of little infants. They had eyes and legs and arms. Whoever sniffed the fruit could live three hundred and sixty years. Whoever ate the fruit could live four thousand seven hundred years.

That day, thirty of the magic infant fruit were ripe. Reality Spirit took two fruit to visit a friend. He left two little spirits named Wind and Moon to watch his temple.

Before leaving he told them, "Today a kind monk will pass by our temple. You should treat him to two of our magic infant fruits."

"What is his name?" asked Wind.

"He is Monk Tang from Chang An," replied the spirit. "Although he is good, his disciples are not. Don't let them know about the magic fruit."

Soon Monk Tang and his disciples climbed up to Longevity Temple. Carved wooden columns supported a yellow tiled roof.

"This temple is beautiful," exclaimed Sandy. "Let's go in and look around."

Wind and Moon greeted the four at the door and showed them around the temple.

But soon Monk Tang was tired. They had done a lot of climbing that morning. He asked Wind, "May we use your stove? We have some rice in our sack and would like to cook it for lunch."

When Wind agreed, Monk Tang asked Monkey to take the horse out to graze while Sandy and Piggy fixed lunch.

Monk Tang sat down to rest as the others went about their work. Wind took the opportunity to ask, "Are you Monk Tang from Chang An?"

"Why, yes. How did you know my name?"

"Our master, Reality Spirit said you would stop by today," Wind replied. "Take a rest, we'll be back in a minute." Wind picked up a golden pole. Moon took a red lacquered plate and covered it with silk. The two went into the court yard to pick the magic fruit.

Wind climbed on the tree and tapped two fruit lightly with his golden pole. Moon caught the fruit on his lacquered plate.

They returned inside and respectfully presented Monk Tang with the fruit, saying, "Please taste our master's specialty, magic fruit."

Monk Tang gasped in surprise. "These aren't fruits. They are infants. I can't eat them."

"They are magic infant fruit."

"There isn't a famine now. How can you eat babies?" returned Monk Tang in horror.

"They may look like babies, but they grew on a tree."

"Please, don't lie," gasped Monk Tang. "Babies don't grow on trees. Take those things away."

The magic fruits had to be eaten soon after they were picked or they would rot. Wind and Moon saw that Monk Tang would not eat the fruit, so they took the fruit back to their own room to eat.

Their room was next to the kitchen. Piggy was in the kitchen boiling rice. As they sat on their beds and talked and ate, Piggy could hear everything. He heard how precious the fruit were. He heard how they used a golden pole to get the fruit from the tree. He heard how Monk Tang refused to eat the magic fruit. Piggy's mouth drooled with expectation. He poked his head out the kitchen door and looked for Monkey.

Monkey had just tied the horse to a tree and was about to sit down beside it.

"Pssst, over here!" Piggy beckoned with his hand.

"What?" asked Monkey walking up to the kitchen door. "Don't tell me there isn't enough to eat."

"There's magic fruit in this temple," Piggy said mysteriously. "It's something you've never seen."

"I've been all over the world and all over heaven. I've seen everything," retorted Monkey.

"Have you seen magic infant fruit?"

108

"No, I've never seen them, but I've heard if some-body eats one of them, he'll be an immortal."

"They are here in this court yard," Piggy grinned as he told Monkey what he had overheard. "You are quicker than I am. Why don't you pick a few for us to try?"

"Easy," cried Monkey as he was about to leave.

"Wait. You need a golden pole," reminded Piggy.

Monkey chanted a spell and turned invisible. He sneaked into the room where Wind and Moon were talking and stole the golden pole.

Then Monkey hurried to the court yard. He squeaked open the butterfly doors and found himself in a flower garden. He walked through the flower gar-den and found another set of doors. When he passed through these, he found himself in a vegetable garden. There was another door. When he opened this last door he found a gigantic tree.

The tree was one hundred yards tall and as thick as a building. Scattered throughout the large palm leaves were magic fruit that looked like little babies.

Monkey grinned in delight. "Piggy was telling the truth."

With a nimble leap, Monkey jumped on a branch, took the golden pole and aimed at one fruit. The fruit

tumbled to the ground. Monkey jumped off the branch and went to pick it up. But the fruit had disappeared.

"Strange," Monkey said to himself. "The fruit couldn't have walked away. Where did it go?"

"Ground spirit," Monkey called. "Did you take my fruit and eat it?"

A thin, old spirit appeared before Monkey. "Please don't blame me. I don't dare touch Reality Spirit's magic fruit. Of course I would not eat one of those precious things."

"Well, what happened to the fruit I just knocked off the tree?"

"Remember," said the old spirit, "you have to catch the fruit on a red lacquered plate covered with silk."

"Since it's not your fault, you can leave now," Monkey said with a wave of his hand.

As the spirit disappeared, Monkey climbed back on a branch. With one hand he pulled up the end of his shirt and made a little basket. With the other hand, he struck at fruit. Before the fruits dropped to the ground, he caught them in his shirt.

When he had three magic fruit, Monkey returned to the kitchen.

"Did you get any?" asked Piggy, his mouth drooling with expectation.

"Of course," laughed Monkey. "One for each of us."

Piggy swallowed his in one gulp and watched hungrily as Sandy and Monkey nibbled at theirs.

"Monkey," said Piggy, "Get me another. One wasn't enough."

"Eating magic fruit isn't like eating rice," exclaimed Monkey. "Tasting it is good enough. You don't eat until you are full."

At this point, Wind and Moon walked into the kitchen to get some water for Monk Tang's tea. They heard Monkey and Piggy talking about eating magic fruit.

"Oh, no," said Wind as he backed out of the kitchen. "I think those monks ate some of our magic fruit."

"The golden pole isn't on the wall," cried Moon as he peaked into the bedroom. "We had better check the garden to see if everything is all right."

The two rushed into the garden and counted the fruits on the tree.

"Twenty-two," declared Moon.

"There should be twenty-six. Reality Spirit took two and we took two," said Wind. "That means four are missing."

Wind and Moon charged back into the temple cursing Monk Tang.

"Rat-headed robber!"

"Stinking monk!"

"Mindless idiot!"

Monk Tang was puzzled.

"What's the matter little ones?" he asked soothing-ly. "If something is wrong, just tell me."

"What's there to tell. You stole our magic infant fruit," cried Wind.

"What is infant fruit?" asked Monk Tang.

"We gave you two to eat, that's what," retorted Moon.

"You offered me one to eat and I didn't take it. I would not steal it," replied Monk Tang. "You shouldn't blame an innocent person."

"Well, if you didn't steal them, then your disciples did," shouted Wind.

"Maybe, maybe," Monk Tang said thoughtfully. "But don't yell. I'll ask them to replace the fruit for you."

"Replace!" shrieked Moon. "Magic infant fruit are priceless. You can't use money to pay for them.

Monk Tang called, "Monkey, Piggy, Sandy, come here. Which one of you stole some magic fruit? They are fruit that look like little babies."

Piggy looked around innocently and replied, "It wasn't me. I have never seen such things."

Monkey could not help laughing at Piggy's attempt to hide his guilt.

"You're laughing," Wind pointed at Monkey. "You must have eaten the fruit."

"Can't I laugh?" Monkey shot back angrily. "Just because I laugh doesn't mean I'm to blame."

Monk Tang said hastily, "We are monks. We cannot lie and steal. If you did eat those fruits, admit it and beg forgiveness."

Monkey knew Monk Tang was correct, so he admitted to taking three fruit at Piggy's suggestion.

"I'm sorry to have taken your fruit," he apologized to Wind and Moon.

"You *stole* four!" cried Wind. "Four, not three. You're still lying."

Monkey was furious. He thought to himself, "I said I was sorry and that idiot still curses me. Well, he just won't have any fruit left at all."

Monkey plucked a hair and chanted a spell. A fake Monkey King stood by Monk Tang and endured the cursing of Wind and Moon. Monkey himself went into the court yard and with a few whacks of his magic rod, knocked the magic tree over. All the magic fruit rolled into the ground and disappeared.

Wind and Moon ranted and raved at Monk Tang for over an hour. Monk Tang listened patiently.

After awhile, Wind said, "This monk doesn't yell back. Maybe he didn't eat our fruit. Let's go back to the tree and count the fruit again."

When Wind and Moon returned to the court yard to count the fruit, they were shocked to find the fruit tree had been toppled over and not a single fruit remained.

"Reality Spirit is going to be mad at us," moaned Wind. "What shall we do?"

"We need to capture those monks," said Moon. "But we'll never do it two against four."

Moon thought awhile before saying, "Let's go back and tell them that we were wrong. We had miscounted the fruit. We will apologize and cook them a few dishes for dinner. While they are eating, we will lock the doors. Then we can let Reality Spirit take care of them when he returns."

Wind agreed to the plan.

The two little spirits waited until Monk Tang, Monkey, Piggy and Sandy were in the main temple eating dinner, then they sneaked outside and locked the doors.

Then Wind yelled, "You greedy bald-headed thieves. You stole our fruits and destroyed our fruit tree. Just wait until our master gets home!"

Chapter 12

Reality Spirit Revenges

Monk Tang shook his head in exasperation. "You naughty Monkey. You ate their fruit. You should let them curse us awhile. Why did you complicate matters by destroying their tree?"

"Master, don't worry. Wait until they sleep. I'll get us out of here," Monkey replied calmly.

"But they've chained and locked all the doors," said Sandy.

"I've got plenty of magic tricks," Monkey laughed.

Piggy grimaced, "You can change into a mosquito and fly out, but what about the rest of us?"

"Wait and see," said Monkey.

When the moon had risen high in the sky and the temple was quiet, Monkey took the needle from his ear, swung it until it was as big as a broom handle and pointed it at the locked door. He chanted an "Unlocking Spell" and suddenly the door squeaked open.

Monkey helped Monk Tang onto the horse. He lead the horse to the main path and let Sandy take the reign. Piggy picked up the luggage and followed in the rear.

"Go quickly," Monkey urged, "While I fix those two little servants."

"Don't harm them," warned Monk Tang.

"I won't," returned Monkey.

He crept back to the window of Wind and Moon and took out two sleeping bugs. He pushed the bugs in through a crack in a window and let them circle over the heads of Wind and Moon. Soon both were snoring like thunder.

In a leap, Monkey had caught up with the others.

The four sped along the mountain path all night. By dawn, Monk Tang was yawning. "Let's rest. I didn't sleep the whole night."

Monk Tang got off the horse. He sat under a pine tree, crossed his legs and rested. Sandy napped on the luggage. Piggy curled up by a rock.

The next morning when Reality Spirit returned to Longevity Temple, he found the doors wide open. Wind and Moon were snoring so loudly that no amount of calling and shaking would wake them. Finally,

Reality Spirit poured water over their heads and they opened their eyes.

Wind sobbed as the tears rolled down his checks, "Master, that kind monk from Chang An is really a thief."

"What? Did he beat you?"

"No, but his disciple Monkey destroyed your magic fruit tree."

Reality Spirit took one look at his garden and saw the toppled tree.

"Can you recognize them?" he asked Wind and Moon.

When both nodded, he took them on a cloud with him. They flew around until Moon spotted Monk Tang sitting beneath a pine tree.

Reality Spirit changed into the shape of an old priest and landed on the ground. He walked up to Monk Tang and asked, "Where are you from?"

Monk Tang greeted the priest with a bow, "I am from Chang An. I am on my way west to Thunder Temple."

"Did you pass through my temple, Longevity Temple?"

Monkey knew the old priest was Reality Spirit who had come to capture them. Monkey pulled out his magic rod and dashed toward the old man.

But Reality Spirit was too quick. He waved the long sleeves of his robe and chanted a spell. Suddenly Monk Tang, Monkey, Piggy, Sandy, the horse and luggage were all sitting inside Reality Spirit's sleeve.

Piggy hacked wildly with his hoe in an attempt to escape. But Reality Spirit's arm was as hard as iron. Nothing could hurt it.

In a flash, Reality Spirit brought them back to Longevity Temple and plucked them out of his sleeve one by one. First he took out Monk Tang and tied him to a pillar. Next was Monkey, then Piggy and Sandy.

When all of them were secured to posts, he called out a strong servant and handed him a whip made of dragon skin.

"Beat them to avenge my Magic Fruit Tree," cried Reality Spirit.

"Which one first?" asked the servant.

"Monk Tang," declared Reality Spirit.

Monkey gulped as he thought to himself, "Master can't take a beating. One whip and he'll die."

Monkey cried out, "I stole the fruit. I ate the fruit and I destroyed the fruit tree. Whip me first."

Reality Spirit laughed, "If you insist." He ordered the servant to whip Monkey thirty times.

Monkey saw the whip coming toward his legs. He chanted a spell and changed his legs into iron. The thirty strokes of the whip did not hurt Monkey at all.

After Monkey was beaten, Reality Spirit called out, "It's Monk Tang's turn."

Monkey declared, "When I stole your fruit, my master did not know. It was my fault. As a disciple, I should take his whippings."

Reality Spirit thought to himself, "That Monkey may be a thief, but he sure is good to his master."

"Okay," he ordered the servant, "Whip Monkey thirty more times."

By the time that was finished, it was already growing dark. Reality Spirit and his servant went in to rest for the night.

Monk Tang sighed, "The three of you steal fruit and I have to suffer with you."

"I took your beating," said Monkey.

"But it is uncomfortable to be tied to this post all day," returned Monk Tang.

"Wait until everyone is asleep," said Monkey. "I have a plan."

About midnight, Monkey chanted a spell to himself. He shrunk in half and slipped out through the ropes. He ran over to untie Monk Tang.

"Don't forget me," cried Sandy.

Monkey quickly untied Sandy and Piggy. He told Sandy to escape with Monk Tang.

"Piggy," he cried. "Dig up four willow trees from the stream."

"For what?" asked Piggy.

"Don't ask questions," retorted Monkey. "Hurry up and do as I say."

Piggy dug up a willow tree and dragged it back. Monkey ripped off all the leaves. Then he tied it to the post with rope. When all four willow trees were tied to posts, he bit his tongue until it bled, sprayed blood onto the trees and shouted "Change!"

One tree turned into Monk Tang; another became Monkey, a third Piggy and the last Sandy. The wooden dummies could talk and laugh. They looked like real.

Monkey and Piggy then hurried out of Longevity Temple and caught up with Monk Tang and Sandy.

The next morning Reality Spirit ordered his servant to whip Monk Tang. The servant went up to Monk Tang's dummy and said, "It is your turn."

"Okay," answered the willow tree.

After thirty lashes, Reality Spirit declared it was Piggy's turn.

The servant went up to Piggy's dummy and said, "It is your turn."

"Okay," answered the willow tree.

When Piggy's dummy was finished, Sandy's dummy was also whipped thirty times.

When the servant started whipping Monkey's dummy, the real Monkey shuddered in pain.

"They whipped me sixty times yesterday," he said to the others. "I didn't think they'd whip my dummy today. I can really feel it. I can't hold up the trick any longer." Monkey then chanted a spell to himself.

Suddenly the servant at Longevity Temple discovered he was whipping a willow tree.

Reality Spirit laughed coldly. "That Monkey King truly knows a lot of tricks. But I'll get him yet."

He jumped on a cloud and flew west. Indeed he spotted Monk Tang and the other hurrying away from his temple.

Piggy spotted him first. "Watch out everyone," he cried, "Reality Spirit is after us."

Monkey grabbed his rod. Piggy clutched his hoe. Sandy wielded his cane. All three attacked Reality Spirit at once.

But with one sweep of his long sleeve, Reality Spirit had captured all three inside. He put Monk Tang and the horse in his other sleeve.

He flew back to Longevity Temple and tied each one to a pine tree. He ordered his servants to bring out a huge cauldron of oil. Beneath it he lit a flame and waited until the oil started boiling.

"Look, Piggy," laughed Monkey. "A pot. They are going to feed us."

"If we are going to die, it's better to die on a full stomach," Piggy agreed.

"We are going to fry you alive," cried Reality Spirit.

"I haven't had a hot bath in months," declared Monkey. "Now is as good a time as any."

Monkey knew he could not survive in boiling oil. He looked around for a replacement. At the bottom of the steps he saw a stone lion. He chanted a spell and traded places with the lion. The stone lion was now tied to a stake in the form of Monkey.

"The oil is boiling," cried Reality Spirit. "Throw Monkey in."

Four servants went to pick up Monkey, but they couldn't lift him. Two more came to help. "This monkey may be small," complained one servant, "but he sure is heavy."

Finally, twenty servants were able to lift Monkey and throw him in the pot. Oil splattered onto the faces of the servants, causing huge blisters.

"The pot is leaking," cried a servant at the side.

Everyone rushed forward to see what was going on. They found a stone lion had cracked the pot.

"Forget Monkey," cried Reality Spirit in anger. "Let's just fry Monk Tang."

Monkey thought to himself, "Master will die if he's put in that boiling oil."

"No, no," declared Monkey rushing up to Reality Spirit. "You can boil me. I just had to go to the bathroom. I was afraid if I went in your oil, your food wouldn't taste very good."

With a cold laugh, Reality Spirit grabbed Monkey. "I know you have seventy-two magical tricks, but you're not leaving Longevity Temple until you compensate for my magic fruit tree."

"Why didn't you say so earlier?" grinned Monkey. "I can resurrect your tree. If you had asked me, you could have saved a lot of time."

"If you really have the ability," said Reality Spirit, "I'll forgive you."

"I'll resurrect your tree if you let my Master go," replied Monkey.

"But how will you do that?" asked Monk Tang.

"I'll get help from fairies in heaven," said Monkey as he left Longevity Temple.

Soon he was standing in front of the three Star Fairies of Heaven. They were sitting calmly under the shade of an old pine tree, playing chess.

"Help me," said Monkey. "I need a spell to resurrect Reality Spirit's magic fruit tree."

The first Star Fairy exclaimed, "The magic fruit tree! If that has been damaged, nothing can help you."

"If you injured a bird or a beast, we have magic medicine to help," replied the second Star Fairy. "But that magic infant tree is so precious, our medicine won't help it."

"Try Fairy Noble," urged the third, "He might be able to help."

Monkey bowed to the three Star Fairies and headed for Fairy Noble's palace. It was a large marble building surrounded by sparkling pools.

A fairy servant at the gate cried, "Monkey King, what are you doing here? My master has no peaches for you to steal."

At this point, Fairy Noble floated out and asked, "May I help you?"

"Yes," replied Monkey. "I need medicine to resurrect Reality Spirit's magic fruit tree."

"Oh my!" exclaimed Fairy Nobel. "*What* did you do to harm that tree!"

He then added, "I have medicine to help injured people, but nothing to help a magic tree. I'm sorry, but you'll have to go elsewhere."

Monkey flew to the far corner of heaven and knocked on Goddess Pusa's door.

"Help me," he said. "Monk Tang is captured by Reality Spirit. I need to resurrect the magic fruit tree so I can free my Master."

Goddess Pusa picked up a jar of heavenly dew and said, "Show me the tree."

Monkey grinned to himself, "If nobody else can help, Goddess Pusa always can."

When the two arrived at Longevity Temple, Reality Spirit gasped as he fell to his knees and bowed, "Goddess, what brings you to my humble abode?"

"Monk Tang, my disciple, has been detained here," answered the Goddess, "I've come to repair your fallen tree, so he can continue on his journey west."

Goddess Pusa sprinkled heavenly dew on the fallen tree and in seconds it stood upright, with twenty-three magic infant fruit on its branches.

Reality Spirit took out the lacquered plate and golden pole and knocked off ten fruit for a magic fruit party to send Monk Tang on the rest of his journey.

When Monk Tang saw that the infant-shaped
fruits really did grow on a tree, he joined everyone in
enjoying them.